Acting Edition

Click, Clack, Boo!

A Tricky Treat

Adapted by Ernie Nolan

Music by David Weinstein

Lyrics by David Weinstein and Ernie Nolan

Based on the book by Doreen Cronin and Betsy Lewin

FOR PRODUCTION INQUIRIES

UNITED STATES AND CANADA
info@concordtheatricals.com
1-866-979-0447

UNITED KINGDOM AND EUROPE
licensing@concordtheatricals.co.uk
020-7054-7298

Each title is subject to availability from Concord Theatricals Corp.,
depending upon country of performance. Please be aware that *CLICK,
CLACK, BOO!* may not be licensed by Concord Theatricals Corp. in
your territory. Professional and amateur producers should contact the
nearest Concord Theatricals Corp. office or licensing partner to verify
availability.

No one shall make any changes in this title(s) for the purpose of production. No part of this book may be reproduced, stored in a retrieval system, scanned, uploaded, or transmitted in any form, by any means, now known or yet to be invented, including mechanical, electronic, digital, photocopying, recording, videotaping, or otherwise, without the prior written permission of the publisher. No one shall share this title(s), or any part of this title(s), through any social media or file hosting websites.

For all inquiries regarding motion picture, television, online/digital and other media rights, please contact Concord Theatricals Corp.

THIRD-PARTY MATERIALS USE NOTE

Licensees are solely responsible for obtaining formal written permission from copyright owners to use copyrighted third-party materials (e.g., incidental music not provided in connection with a performance license, artworks, logos) in the performance of this play and are strongly cautioned to do so. If no such permission is obtained by the licensee, then the licensee must use only original materials and materials that the licensee owns and controls. Licensees are solely responsible and liable for clearances of all third-party copyrighted materials, and shall indemnify the copyright owners of the play(s) and their licensing agent, Concord Theatricals Corp., against any costs, expenses, losses and liabilities arising from the use of such copyrighted third-party materials by licensees. For music, please contact the appropriate music licensing authority in your territory for the rights to any incidental music not provided in connection with a performance license.

IMPORTANT BILLING AND CREDIT REQUIREMENTS

If you have obtained performance rights to this title, please refer to your licensing agreement for important billing and credit requirements.

CLICK, CLACK, BOO! premiered at Nashville Children's Theatre in Nashville, Tennessee on October 1, 2022. The performance was directed by Ernie Nolan, with music direction by Kelsi Fulton, the production stage manager was Rachael Silverman, and the assistant stage manager was Abby Austin. The cast was as follows:

DARLENE . . . . Piper Jones

CLARISSA . . . . Erika Johnson

CHICK . . . . Eve Petty

FARMER BROWN . . . . Dustin Davis

CHARACTERS

DARLENE – a Bea Arthur-esque wise-talking duck

CLARISSA – a party-loving cow

CHICK – an enthusiastic and naïve chicken

FARMER BROWN – a cantankerous old farmer

SETTING

Farmer Brown's barnyard. The present.

TIME

Evening, a time when friendly thrills and chills can occur.

AUTHOR'S NOTES

In addition to touring, the original production celebrated the fall season and was produced outdoors. Audiences sat on hay bales and participated in fall activities before and after the performance giving it a pumpkin patch/fall festival vibe. Feel free to play with your own autumn environment.

MUSIC NUMBERS

[MUSIC NO. 01 – HALLOWEEN HOP]

(A barnyard. As music starts, CLARISSA [the cow], CHICK [the chicken], and DARLENE [the duck] appear, each carrying an item for a celebration.)

DARLENE.
I BROUGHT A PUMPKIN

CHICK.
I BROUGHT BALLOONS

CLARISSA.
I BROUGHT THE SNACKS

CLARISSA, CHICK & DARLENE.
WOW! LOOK AT THE MOON!

DARLENE.
YOU LOOK FOR MONSTERS

CHICK.
YOU LOOK FOR GHOSTS

CLARISSA.
I THINK THE THREE OF US WILL MAKE PERFECT HOSTS

CLARISSA, CHICK & DARLENE.
IT'S OUR FAVORITE TIME OF YEAR
WHEN THE AIR IS CRISP AND THE NIGHT IS CLEAR
WE'RE GONNA MAKE THE BARNYARD BOP
TONIGHT AT OUR HALLOWEEN HOP!
HOP HOP HOP HOP
HALLA HALLA HALLA HALLA HALLOWEEN HOP
WE'RE GONNA MAKE THE BARNYARD BOP
TONIGHT AT OUR HALLOWEEN HOP!
DANCE BREAK!

CLARISSA.

I'LL BOB FOR APPLES

CHICK.

I'LL CHASE THE BATS

DARLENE.

THIS HAPPY HORROR HOLIDAY IS WHERE IT'S AT!

CLARISSA.

THE JACK O'LANTERNS

DARLENE.

ARE ALL AGLOW

CLARISSA, CHICK & DARLENE.

ALL THE TRICK OR TREATERS ARE STARTING TO SHOW
EVERY CREATURE IN THE YARD WILL BE JITTER BUGGIN'
AND STOMPIN' HARD
WE'RE GONNA MAKE THE BARNYARD BOOM BAM BOP
TONIGHT AT OUR HALLOWEEN HOP!

ALRIGHT NOW!

HOP HOP HOP HOP
HALLA HALLA HALLA HALLA HALLOWEEN HOP
WE'RE GONNA MAKE THE BARNYARD BOO BOP!
TONIGHT AT OUR HALLOWEEN HOP

LISTEN CLOSELY NOW!
ALL THE PIGS IN THE STY
AND THE BIRDS PASS ON BY
ALL THE DUCKS AND CATTLE WELL,
THEY'RE GONNA MAKE A RATTLE
WE'RE ALL GONNA JUMP AND JIVE!
EV'RYBODY SING!

HOP HOP HOP HOP
HALLA HALLA HALLA HALLA HALLOWEEN HOP
WE'RE GONNA MAKE THE BARNYARD BOP
WE'LL BE DANCIN' TILL WE CANNOT STOP

THIS SPOOKY SCARY STRANGE PARTY'S
GONNA POP!

CHICK.
CANDY AT HALLOWEEN!

DARLENE.
COSTUMES AT HALLOWEEN

CLARISSA.
FRIENDSHIP AT HALLOWEEN

CLARISSA, CHICK & DARLENE.
FRIGHT'NING FUN AT HALLOWEEN!
WE LOVE HALLOWEEN
TONIGHT AT OUR HALLOWEEN
BOO! HOP!

CLARISSA. I've been waiting all year for this!

CHICK. To sing an opening number?

CLARISSA. The annual Halloween Hop, Chick.

DARLENE. It's the social event of the season.

CLARISSA. It's why I made my special party dip.

DARLENE. And I brought a pumpkin.

CHICK. So that's why I brought balloons!

DARLENE. We sang a whole song about it. How could you forget why you brought them?

CHICK. I knew they were for something.

DARLENE. That "something" is the perfect accompaniment for all of the contests in store...

CLARISSA. Like the loudest scream...

DARLENE. The most spirited participant...

CLARISSA. The best costume...

CHICK. And weight lifting!

CLARISSA & DARLENE. Weight lifting?!?!?

CHICK. Hello! It's Halloween. It's time to get "pumpkin iron"!

*(Laughing at her own joke, **CHICK** does a series of bodybuilding poses.)*

Did you hear about the bodybuilding vegetable?

CLARISSA & DARLENE. No.

CHICK. He was a muscle sprout.

(Continuing to laugh and strike poses.)

You know why skeletons can't lift weights?

CLARISSA & DARLENE. No why?

CHICK. They are all bone and no muscle!

*(**CHICK** laughs at her wit, **CLARISSA** and **DARLENE** try to take in the situation.)*

DARLENE. You thought of those all on your own, didn't you, Chick?

CHICK. Yep. And there are plenty more where they came from.

DARLENE. Now that's frightening!

CLARISSA. There'll be plenty of time for treats *and* tricks later. Especially for the winner of the costume contest. The winner gets a special prize.

DARLENE. Clarissa, it looks like the whole barnyard got our invitations. Everyone is starting to arrive.

CLARISSA. Hey there sheep!

*(Pointing to a section of the **AUDIENCE**.)*

Can I hear a "Ba-ba hello!" from the sheep over on this side of the barnyard? "Ba-ba hello!" on the count of three? Ready? One – two – three.

AUDIENCE. Ba-Ba Hello!

DARLENE. Wonderful. Now can I hear a "Nibble, nibble ya'll!" from the mice over on this side of the barnyard? "Nibble, nibble y'all!" on the count of three? Ready? One – two – three.

AUDIENCE. Nibble, nibble y'all!

CHICK. Wow! Now if I can get a "Hee-haw-hee-haw-hee" from the alpacas...

DARLENE. Alpacas?!?!?!

CHICK. A South American mammal similar to, but often confused with, the llama.

DARLENE. There aren't any alpacas on Farmer Brown's farm.

CHICK. We really outta look into fixing that.

CLARISSA. But there *are* cats. Now can I hear a "Meow-meow hey!" from the cats over on this side of the barnyard? "Meow meow hey" on the count of three? Ready? One – two –

FARMER BROWN. *(Offstage.)* What in tarnation is going on out there?!?!?

CLARISSA, CHICK & DARLENE. Farmer Brown!

DARLENE. He doesn't sound happy. Let's make ourselves scarce.

> (**DARLENE** *and* **CLARISSA** *move to hide.* **CHICK** *stands confused.)*

CLARISSA. What are you doing?

CHICK. I don't know how to make myself scarce?

DARLENE. Hide!

CHICK. That first. Then I'll learn how to make myself scarce second.

*(**CHICK** finds a place to hide, just as **FARMER BROWN** bursts onto the scene.)*

FARMER BROWN. Now what's makin' y'all bumfuzzled…

*(**FARMER BROWN** looks around, sees that no one is there.)*

Heavens to betsy. Something's cattywampus.

CLARISSA, CHICK & DARLENE. *(Revealing themselves quickly from hiding.)* Cattywampus?

FARMER BROWN. Cattywampus.

(Noticing the things the group brought for the party.)

Balloons…a pumpkin…special party dip?!?!? That can mean only one thing.

CHICK. *(Standing up, quickly, from hiding.)* A good time!

FARMER BROWN. A Halloween party!

*(**DARLENE** and **CLARISSA** encourage **CHICK** to return to her hiding spot.)*

[MUSIC NO. 02 – NONSENSE TO ME]

(spoken in rhythm) I… I… I…
I DON'T LIKE HALLOWEEN PARTIES
THERE'S NO NEED TO DISCUSS
THEY'RE NOISY, LOUD, WITH SUCH A CROWD
I DON'T GET ALL THE FUSS
NO, I DON'T LIKE HALLOWEEN PARTIES
DON'T NEED DRESS-UP CLOTHES
THOSE ITCHY, SCRATCHY RAGS
A BAN! I DO PROPOSE!
WITCHES GIVE ME NIGHTMARES
SKELETONS SHAKE MY BONES
SPIDERS, BATS, GHOSTS, AND BLACK CATS

I LIKE IT ON MY OWN!

NO! I DON'T LIKE HALLOWEEN FUN
OR CHRISTMAS JAMBOREES,
A GALA CELEBRATION, OR HANG, AND MOST FESTIVITIES
A BIRTHDAY GATH'RIN AND ALL THAT BLATH'RIN
IT'S ALL NONSENSE TO ME!

> *(Grumpy, boogie dance break.* **FARMER BROWN** *tries to dispose of the party things as* **CLARISSA**, **CHICK**, *and* **DARLENE** *save decorations and such without him knowing.)*

FARMER BROWN.	CLARISSA, CHICK & DARLENE
WEREWOLVES GIVE ME GOOSEBUMPS	OOH
	GOOSEBUMPS
ZOMBIES TURN ME TO STONE	OOH
	TO STONE!

FARMER BROWN.

VAMPIRES DON'T MAKE SENSE TO ME
I LIKE IT ON MY OWN!

CLARISSA, CHICK & DARLENE.

NO SIR!

FARMER BROWN.

SO THAT'S A NO FOR HALLOWEEN PARTIES
SHINDIG, BASH, SOIRÉE
A COFFEE CLUTCH? THAT'S WAY TOO MUCH
I'LL TAKE A PASS CAN'T YOU SEE
IT'S UTTER BUNK TO ME!

CLARISSA, CHICK & DARLENE.

UTTER BUNK!

FARMER BROWN.

TAKE THAT HOGWASH OUT TO SEA!

CLARISSA, CHICK & DARLENE.
> TAKE THAT HOGWASH!

FARMER BROWN.
> THAT BALDERDASH SHOULD GO OUT WITH THE TRASH
> 'CAUSE IT'S ALL NONSENSE TO ME!!!!
> GOBELDY GOOK, POPPY COCK, FIDDLESTICKS, TOMMYROT
> ALL NONSENSE TO ME!

Now I don't know which of you critters thinks I'll have anything to do with this Halloween Hooey...

> *(***CHICK*** *raises her hand while hiding.* ***CLARISSA*** *and* ***DARLENE*** *lower it.)*

But I won't. Not this year. Or next. Or any in the future. I don't like Halloween parties, because...

> *(***CLARISSA, CHICK*** *and* ***DARLENE*** *lean in to see what the answer is.)*

I don't like Halloween.

> *(***CLARISSA, CHICK*** *and* ***DARLENE*** *gasp.)*

> *(Dramatic musical tag.)*

FARMER BROWN. If anybody, or any animal, thinks, I'm attending a Halloween party this evening, they're barkin' up the wrong tree. My RSVP is "No thank you!" It would take something pretty spectacular for me to attend, 'cause the only thing I will be attending is bed!

> *(They silently react disappointed.)*

Parties are full of contests and I never win...not the most spirited participant...or the best costume...or weight lifting.

CLARISSA & DARLENE. Weight lifting?!?!?

FARMER BROWN. Let's face it. My average leg workout is doin' diddly squat. Now it's time to finish up the day, so I can hit the hay.

(**FARMER BROWN** *exits to finish his chores.*)

DARLENE. But this isn't right. How can Farmer Brown not like Halloween parties? If anyone deserves a break…

CLARISSA. Or an excuse to let loose…

DARLENE. It's Farmer Brown.

CHICK. This is just like the skeleton who didn't go to the dance?

DARLENE. It is.

CHICK. Sure. He had no *body* to go with.

DARLENE. That was another original, wasn't it?

CHICK. Can you tell?

DARLENE. Let me tell you…

CLARISSA. *(Interrupting.)* That Farmer Brown doesn't know the true meaning of Halloween.

CHICK. Exactly! He doesn't realize that it's about candy.

DARLENE. No, no, no, Chick. That's a common misperception. There's so much more to this unique holiday. You see…

(*Academic music begins to play.**)

DARLENE. In ancient times, Halloween observed the end of the harvest. It has now grown into a worldwide phenomenon that inspires the creative mind, extols

---

* Performance Materials for *Click, Clack, Boo!* do not include music for this moment. A license to produce *Click, Clack, Boo!* does not include a performance license for any third-party or copyrighted recordings. Licensees should create their own.

storytelling, produces arts and crafts, and stimulates creative role play.

(*The academic music finishes.*)

CHICK. (*Shocked.*) Hold it right there.

DARLENE. Yes, Chick?

CHICK. Are you telling me it's *not* about the candy?!?

DARLENE. Candy is part of the celebration, but Halloween is really about taking time to celebrate and have fun, no matter the age.

CLARISSA. And if I might add...

DARLENE. You may, Clarissa.

CLARISSA. It's about celebrating *together*.

DARLENE. (*Putting a hand out for* **DARLENE** *and* **CHICK**.) With friends.

CHICK. Ohhhhh. Now I get it.

DARLENE. The importance of Halloween?

CHICK. No. Why demons and ghouls hang out.

CLARISSA. Why is that?

CHICK. Because demons are a ghoul's best friend.

(**CHICK** *delivers a "HA-CHA" ending.*)

DARLENE. You spent a lot of time on that one, didn't you, Chick?

CHICK. How could you tell?

(*Gets an idea.*)

Oh. Oh. Oh. You don't think...

CLARISSA & DARLENE. Yes?

CHICK. That Farmer Brown thinks...

CLARISSA & DARLENE. Yes?

CHICK. That he doesn't have any friends to celebrate with.

> (**CLARISSA** *and* **DARLENE** *look at each other in disbelief.*)

DARLENE & CLARISSA. Impossible!

CHICK. Is it?

DARLENE & CLARISSA. Impossible!

CHICK. Or is it?

DARLENE & CLARISSA. Impossible!

DARLENE. The farm is full of his friends. Don't you think so, Clarissa?

CLARISSA. Of course, Darlene! We're his friends.

DARLENE. And the mice are his friends.

CLARISSA. And the sheep are his friends.

CHICK. And the alpacas?

DARLENE. There aren't any alpacas, Chick.

CHICK. But if there were...

DARLENE. I'm sure they would be his friends too.

CLARISSA. So it's up to us to show Farmer Brown he has friends.

DARLENE. And once that happens, he'll feel differently about Halloween and come to the party.

CHICK. Then maybe finally we'll get some alpacas on the farm!

> (**DARLENE** *and* **CLARISSA** *do a slow head turn to* **CHICK**.)

DARLENE. *(A la Bea Arthur.)* We can only dream, Chick. Only dream.

CHICK. Let's make like a mamma ghost getting into the car!

DARLENE. How do we do that?

CHICK. "Fasten our sheet belts!"

> (**CHICK** *chuckles at her joke and is interrupted by a crash, bang offstage.*)

FARMER BROWN. *(Offstage.)* Confounded window shade!

CLARISSA. If we have any hope of gettin' the party started, then let OPERATION HALLO-PAL commence.

> (**CLARISSA** *and* **DARLENE** *walk away to start,* **CHICK** *stands frozen again,* **CLARISSA** *and* **DARLENE** *turn back.*)

DARLENE. We're starting, Chick.

CHICK. Sorry. Guess I was actin' like a mummy.

DARLENE. How so?

CHICK. I was wrapped up in myself.

> (**CHICK** *celebrates her joke,* **DARLENE** *grabs* **CHICK** *and then huddles with* **CLARISSA** *to create a plan out of Farmer Brown's sight.* **FARMER BROWN** *enters with a giant bowl of candy and a sign, which is not revealed.*)

FARMER BROWN. The shades are drawn.

> *(He sets down the giant bowl of candy.)*

Bowl of candy is out.

> *(He prepares to hang the sign that is still unseen.)*

Now all I want is to…

[MUSIC NO. 03 – TELLIN' YOU]

(CLARISSA, CHICK and DARLENE in Andrew Sisters harmony, unseen by FARMER BROWN. Could be "Oooos" or "Ahhs" or animal noises like cluck, quack, or moo to get into verse.)

CLARISSA, CHICK & DARLENE.
CREAK, CREAK, CREAK, CREAK AT YOUR FEET
CRUNCH, CRUNCH, CRUNCH, CRUNCH AS THEY EAT
TAP, TAP, TAP, TAP WITHOUT END
TELLIN' YOU THAT THEY'RE YOUR FRIEND!

EV'RY DAY YOU'RE WORKIN' OUT HERE IN THE BARNYARD
AND IT FEELS LIKE YOU ARE LA BORIN' ON YOUR OWN
LITTLE DID YOU KNOW THAT YOU HAVE FRIENDS
    AROUND YOU
HERE YOU THOUGHT THAT YOU WERE TOILIN' ALL
    ALONE
DAYS ARE LONG AND NIGHTS ARE DARK OUT ON THE
    FARM
MAKING YOU FEEL COLD AND SMALL
BUT WHEN WE ARE TOGETHER WORKING IS A PLEASURE
WE OUGHT TO FEEL A HUNDRED FEET TALL!
TAKE A TICK HAVE A THINK
THE SOUNDS THAT YOU DISCOVER, THEY ARE ALL IN
    SYNC
IF YOU LISTEN TO WHAT YOUR CHUMS HAVE TO SAY
THEY'RE GONNA TELL YOU PLAINLY THAT THEY'RE HERE
    TO STAY
THE MICE ARE CREAK, CREAK, CREAKIN' AT YOUR FEET
THE SHEEP ARE CRUNCH, CRUNCH, CRUNCHIN' AS THEY EAT
THE CATS ARE TAP, TAP, TAPPIN' WITHOUT END
ALL THE NOISES ON THE FARM YOU'RE HEARIN'
TELLIN' YOU THAT THEY'RE YOUR FRIEND

FARMER BROWN. Sounds like there's a mighty wind tonight. I'm glad I locked the windows.

CLARISSA. Wind?!?! How dare he call our three-part harmony "wind"?

DARLENE. You didn't think we were going to win him over with just one verse did you?

CHICK. Farmer Brown's really acting like a mummy...

CLARISSA. How so?

CHICK. He's afraid to unwind!

DARLENE. Come on. Five-six-seven-eight ...

CLARISSA, CHICK & DARLENE.
> LIVIN' BY YOURSELF CAN MAKE YOU FEEL SO EMPTY
> ABANDONED LIKE A HERMIT CRAB WITHOUT A SHELL
> NO, YOU'RE NOT FORSAKEN
> AND WE ARE NOT MISTAKEN
> AS IF A WIZARD CAST AN UNDERSTANDING SPELL
> ALL THIS CLATTER HAS ONE DESIGN
> OUR HALLOWEEN CANDY CORNS SAY "BE MINE!"
> THE KNOCK, KNOCK, KNOCKIN' CAN FEEL BRAND NEW
> BUT THIS IS HOW THE FLOCK IS DROPPIN' LOVE FOR YOU!
> THE MICE ARE CREAK, CREAK, CREAKIN' AT YOUR FEET
> THE SHEEP ARE CRUNCH, CRUNCH, CRUNCHIN' AS THEY
>   EAT
> THE CATS ARE TAP, TAP, TAPPIN' WITHOUT END
> TELLIN' YOU THE DOUBTS SHOULD START TO
>   DISAPPEARIN'
> TELLIN' YOU A LITTLE SUBTLE ENGINEERIN'
> TELLIN' YOU ALL THE NOISES ON THE FARM YOU'RE
>   HEARIN'
> TELLIN' YOU THAT THEY'RE YOUR FRIEND
> KNOCK, CREAK, CRUNCH, TAP, CLICK, CLACK, BOO!

FARMER BROWN. That's not the wind. It's the dogs. Haven't heard such caterwaulin' like that since the last full moon.

CLARISSA. The nerve. Caterwaulin'?!? This barnyard boogie is totally in tune.

DARLENE. But it's *not* doing the trick.

CHICK. Just like when a vampire has trouble with his house?

DARLENE. It is?

CHICK. Yes. It's a grave problem!

> (**CHICK** *cracks herself up.*)

DARLENE. Let's try it one more time.

[MUSIC NO. 04 – TELLIN' YOU (REPRISE)]

> (*The* **AUDIENCE** *shows* **FARMER BROWN** *how friendly they are through their participation. The animal sound breakdown reaches a rhythmic, barnyard climax.* **DARLENE**, **CLARISSA**, *and* **CHICK** *continue singing.*)

CLARISSA, CHICK & DARLENE.
FARMER BROWN IT'S TIME TO HEAR WHAT WE'RE ALL
   SINGIN'
PHRASE IT ANY WAY YOU WANT, WE CALL YOU MATE
YOU ARE MORE THAN JUST THE AV'RAGE VEGGIE
   PLANTER
WE RESPECT YOU MORE THAN ANY HEAD OF STATE
OUR SONG TO YOU IS MORE THAN DUE
WE ARE VERY DEDICATED THROUGH AND THROUGH
ONE MORE TIME, LET'S TRY IT AGAIN
LET'S MAKE SURE HE CAN HEAR IT AND INCLUDE OUR
   FRIENDS.

DARLENE. We need reinforcements.

CHICK. Like the marines?

DARLENE. No. Like the rest of the barnyard. Mice, we need your help. Farmer Brown needs to hear that *you* are his friends too. When I point to you go…

DARLENE. *(Whatever fun rhythm works.)*
CREAK, CREAK, CREAK,
CREAKIN' AT YOUR FEET
CREAK, CREAK, CREAK,
CREAKIN' AT YOUR FEET

Now you try!

AUDIENCE MICE.
CREAK, CREAK, CREAK,
CREAKIN' AT YOUR FEET.
CREAK, CREAK, CREAK,
CREAKIN' AT YOUR FEET.

CLARISSA. Sheep, we're going to need your help as well.
When I point to you go:
CRUNCH, CRUNCH, CRUNCHITY CRUNCH
CRUNCHIN' AS THEY EAT
CRUNCH, CRUNCH, CRUNCHITY CRUNCH
CRUNCHIN' AS THEY EAT

Now you try!

AUDIENCE SHEEP.
CRUNCH, CRUNCH, CRUNCHITY CRUNCH
CRUNCHIN' AS THEY EAT
CRUNCH, CRUNCH, CRUNCHITY CRUNCH
CRUNCHIN' AS THEY EAT

CHICK. Your turn cats. When I point to you go:
TAPPY, TAPPY, TAPPY
WITHOUT END TIP TAP

Now you try!

AUDIENCE CATS.
TAPPY, TAPPY, TAPPY
WITHOUT END TIP TAP
TAPPY, TAPPY, TAPPY
WITHOUT END TIP TAP

DARLENE. Let's put them all together. 5...6...7...8...

AUDIENCE ANIMALS.
> CREAK, CREAK, CREAK, CREAKIN' AT
>   YOUR FEET
> CRUNCH, CRUNCH, CRUNCHITY CRUNCH. CRUNCHIN' AS
>   THEY EAT
> TAPPY, TAPPY, TAPPY WITHOUT END TIP TAP.
>
> THE MICE ARE CREAK, CREAK, CREAKIN' AT YOUR FEET
> THE SHEEP ARE CRUNCH, CRUNCH, CRUNCHIN' AS THEY EAT
> THE CATS ARE TAP, TAP, TAPPIN' WITHOUT END
> ALL THE NOISES ON THE FARM YOU'RE HEARIN'
> TELLIN' YOU THAT THEY'RE YOUR ...

CHICK. *(Jazz scatting to the animal sound.)*
> CLUCKITY CLUCK, CLUCK, CLUCKY
> CLUCK, CLUCK, CLUCKY CLUCK.

CLARISSA, CHICK & DARLENE.
> TELLIN' YOU ...

DARLENE. *(Jazz scatting to the animal sound.)*
> QUACKY, QUACKY, QUACKITY,
> QUACKITY QUACKY, QUACK.

CLARISSA, CHICK & DARLENE.
> TELLIN' YOU ...

CLARISSA.
> MOOOOOOO!

CLARISSA, CHICK & DARLENE.
> TELLIN' YOU THAT THEY'RE YOUR FRIEND
> CREAK, CRUNCH,
> TAP A FRIEND TO YOU!

> *(On the final button,* **FARMER BROWN** *hangs
> up the sign which says "DO NOT DISTURB"
> and exits.)*

DARLENE. *(Reading the sign.)* Do not disturb.

CHICK. I don't think the plan worked.

CLARISSA. Whatever gave you that idea?

CHICK. The sign.

DARLENE. It definitely makes a point.

CLARISSA. Farmer Brown can't spend Halloween alone. He doesn't know what he's missing out on. Like…

CHICK. The alpacas?

DARLENE. Again with the alpacas, Chick?

CHICK. They're a very friendly animal.

DARLENE. We can't give up on OPERATION HALLO-PAL. We just need to work on making our point stronger. Come on, girls. Five-six-seven-eight.

> (**DARLENE**, **CLARISSA**, *and* **CHICK** *begin to reprise the previous song singing it in the direction of Farmer Brown's house* **FARMER BROWN** *lifts up a shade and rings a triangle or blows an air horn. He then barks from the window.)*

FARMER BROWN. Stop all that squawkin'! Now's not the time for a ruckus.

CHICK. *(Proudly.)* Is it time for a Spook-tacular?

FARMER BROWN. It's time to hit the hay.

[MUSIC NO. 05 – HITTIN' THE HAY]

> *(Musical intro starts.)*

END OF THE DAY TAKE THE SHOES OFF MY FEET
I'M READY FOR REST AND DREAMS, SO SWEET.
IT'S MY FAV'RITE PART IN THE DUSK OF THE LIGHT
GETTIN' TO HIT THE HAY AT NIGHT,

> (**FARMER BROWN** *begins to prepare for bed.)*

FARMER BROWN.

> I PUT ON MY PJS
> THE CHOPPERS GET BRUSHED
> I SAY MY PRAYERS.
> 'CAUSE THE BARNYARD IS HUSHED
> IT'S MY FAVORITE PART IN THE DUSK OF LIGHT,
> GETTIN' TO HIT THE HAY AT NIGHT.

> (**FARMER BROWN** *takes off his overalls and reveals a festive union suit.*)

> SIMPLY JUMP INTO BED, TAKE YER FEET OFF THE GROUND
> NOW'S THE TIME FOR LITTLE DOGGIES TO STOP MOVIN'
>   AROUND
> THERE'S NOTHIN' LIKE GETTIN' ALL SNUG AS A BUG
> SIMPLY CUDDLE YOUR BEAR AND GIVE HIM A HUG.

> MY EYELIDS ARE LOW, AND MY MIND'S AWAY
> I'M READY FOR SLUMBER AND A BRAND NEW DAY
> IT'S MY FAV'RITE PART IN THE DUSK OF THE LIGHT
> GETTIN' TO HIT THE HAY AT (SNORE) ...

> (**FARMER BROWN** *has fallen asleep.*)

CLARISSA. He's asleep.

CHICK. Girls, OPERATION HALLO-PAL isn't working. We need to get over to the cemetery.

CLARISSA. Cemetery? Why?

CHICK. There are so many plots there to pick from.

> (**CHICK** *does a "HA-CHA" after her joke.*)

CLARISSA. Chick, no more jokes. We need to be serious.

CHICK. You're right. You're right. We need to be serious... and calm...like skeletons. Nothing gets under their skin.

> (**CHICK** *does another "HA-CHA" after her joke.*)

CLARISSA. *(To* **CHICK.***)* Finished?

CHICK. One more. Knock, knock.

CLARISSA. Who's there?

CHICK. Boo!

CLARISSA. Boo who?

CHICK. Don't cry, Clarissa. I'm sure we'll get Farmer Brown to the party.

>   (**CHICK** *does a final "HA-CHA" after her joke.)*

CLARISSA. Oh really?

FARMER BROWN. *(Snore.)*

CLARISSA. By the sound of that, I'm not so sure.

DARLENE. Do I detect a hint of doubt in your voice, Clarissa?

CLARISSA. It's not a hint. It IS doubt.

DARLENE & CHICK. *(In shock.)* No!

CLARISSA. Yes! Girls, you've heard him. Farmer Brown doesn't want to come to the Halloween Hop. I think we should give…

DARLENE. Don't say it.

CLARISSA. I think we should give…

CHICK. Don't say it.

CLARISSA. I think we should give up.

>   *(****Scary, tense music tag.**** A look of horror comes over **DARLENE** and **CHICK***'s faces.)*

---

* Performance Materials for *Click, Clack, Boo!* do not include music for this moment. A license to produce *Click, Clack, Boo!* does not include a performance license for any third-party or copyrighted recordings. Licensees should create their own.

DARLENE. That's the scariest thing I've heard this Halloween.

CHICK. Is this because of my jokes?

CLARISSA. Its not because of your jokes. OPERATION HALLO-PAL is a joke.

CHICK. But Clarissa, if at first you don't succeed...

(She searches for the completion of the quote.)

If at first you don't succeed...

DARLENE. Try, try again.

CHICK. OK. I will. If at first you don't succeed...you don't succeed...

DARLENE. Clarissa, nothing great ever came that easy. Our efforts to include Farmer Brown are sure to make this the greatest Halloween Hop ever.

CLARISSA. How? We have a problem with no possible solution.

DARLENE. Every problem has a solution. It just hasn't been discovered yet.

CHICK. Like I said, if at first you don't succeed...

DARLENE. Try, try again.

CHICK. OK. This is a lot of pressure. If at first you don't succeed...

DARLENE. You have to face a problem, think of possible solutions, pick one, and test it.

CHICK. If at first you don't succeed...be proud of how hard you are trying.

DARLENE. Not quite.

CLARISSA. But when you've failed like we have?

CHICK. If at first you don't succeed...fluff your feathers and try again.

DARLENE. *(To* **CHICK**.*)* Almost.

(To **CLARISSA**.*)* It's not failing. It's just not finding the solution that works yet.

CHICK. If at first you don't succeed…

[MUSIC NO. 06 – MOVIN' AND GROOVIN']

(Music chord.)

Try…

(Music chord.)

Try…

(Music chord.)

Again!

DARLENE. That's it!
THERE ARE TIMES IN OUR LIVES WHEN WE FACE A BIG
    STUM-B-LIN' BLOCK
YOU GOTTA STEP RIGHT UP AND GIVE IT A GOOD OL'
    KNOCK.
THERE ARE TIMES IN OUT LIVES WHEN WE CAN'T GET IT
    RIGHT
BUT THAT'S THE TIME WE GOTTA PUT UP A FIGHT
THERE ARE TIMES IN OUR LIVES WHEN WE FACE A BIG
    STUM-B-LIN' BLOCK

CHICK.
THERE ARE DAYS WHEN YOU FEEL LIKE YOU JUST CAN'T
    SEEM TO WIN
AND IT SEEMS LIKE EVERYTHING IS A HASSLE AND YOUR
    PATIENCE IS THIN
AND THERE ARE DAYS WHEN YOU KNOW IT'S ALL A MESS,
BUT YOU REALLY WANT TO FIND THE WAY TO SUCCESS
THERE ARE DAYS WHEN YOU FEEL LIKE YOU JUST CAN'T
    SEEM TO WIN

DARLENE.
YOU GOTTA KEEP ON MOVIN’

CHICK.
KEEP ON MOVIN’

DARLENE.
KEEP ON GROOVIN’

CHICK.
KEEP ON GROOVIN’

CLARISSA, CHICK & DARLENE.
A MOVIN’ AND A GROOVIN’
A GROOVIN’ AND A MOVIN’
NO MATTER WHAT COMES YOUR WAY.

CHICK.
FARMER BROWN’S GOT A DOG AND LET ME TELL YOU
THAT DOG WON’T HUNT
HE MISSED OUT ON FUN, ’CAUSE ANY TROUBLE HE WON’T
CONFRONT.
IT’S ALL RIGHT TO FEEL LOW OR FEEL LIKE YOU’RE WORN
OUT
BUT DON’T BE THAT DOG AND JUST SIT THERE AND POUT
FARMER BROWN’S GOT A DOG AND LET ME TELL YOU
THAT DOG WON’T HUNT

DARLENE.
THERE ARE NIGHTS IN THE DARK ALL ALONE WHEN
YOU’RE GRASPIN’ AT STRAWS
DON’T THROW IN THE TOWEL,
LIFT YOUR HEAD AND TAKE A GOOD PAUSE,
THINGS WILL GET BETTER IN THE LIGHT OF DAY
JUST SHAKE OFF THE DARKNESS IT’LL ALL BE OK
THERE ARE NIGHTS IN THE DARK ALL ALONE WHEN
YOU’RE GRASPIN’ AT STRAWS

CHICK.
YOU GOTTA KEEP ON MOVIN’

DARLENE.

KEEP ON MOVIN'

CHICK.

KEEP ON GROOVIN'

DARLENE.

KEEP ON GROOVIN'

CLARISSA, CHICK & DARLENE.

A MOVIN' AND A GROOVIN'

A GROOVIN' AND A MOVIN'

NO MATTER WHAT COMES YOUR WAY

CLARISSA.

OH, YOU'RE RIGHT I'M MOPEY AND SAD I CONCUR.

I'M GONNA TYPE IT CLICK, CLACK, CLICK

ON MY VINTAGE PINK TYPEWRITER

GONNA WORK THROUGH THIS MOOD,

SO IT CAN BE LIKE BEFORE

GONNA TAKE MY TIME FOR STEPS ONE, TWO, THREE,
FOUR

WITH YOU BY MY SIDE, ALL THIS WORK WON'T BE A
CHORE!

CLARISSA.

I GOTTA KEEP ON MOVIN'

DARLENE & CHICK.

KEEP ON MOVIN'

CLARISSA.

I GOTTA KEEP ON GROOVIN'

DARLENE & CHICK.

KEEP ON GROOVIN'

CLARISSA, CHICK & DARLENE.

A MOVIN' AND A GROOVIN'

A GROOVIN' AND A MOVIN'

CLARISSA.

NO MATTER WHAT COMES MY WAY!

CLARISSA, CHICK & DARLENE.

NO MATTER WHAT, NO MATTER WHAT COMES
A MOVIN' AND A GROOVIN'
NO MATTER WHAT COMES OUR WAY
MOVIN' AND A GROOVIN'!

CLARISSA. Girls, I'm so sorry. How could I ever have doubted we would find a solution?

CHICK. Well you know what they say, "When the going gets tough, all you gotta do is sing with your friends."

DARLENE. I like that saying, Chick.

CHICK. Sing with your friends or find a ghost.

DARLENE. A ghost? Why?

CHICK. Well, they make great cheerleaders.

CLARISSA. They do?

CHICK. They're so spirited!

(**CHICK** *does another "HA-CHA" after her joke. All three laugh.*)

DARLENE. That was a good one, Chick.

CHICK. Thanks. I wanted to tell another skeleton pun, but I don't have the guts for it.

(**CHICK** *does another "HA-CHA" after her joke. All three laugh.*)

CLARISSA. All joking aside, let's get movin' and groovin' on what we can we can do next. The night is slipping away, and at this rate we'll run out of time for the Halloween Hop and the loudest scream contest...

DARLENE. And the most spirited participant...

CLARISSA. And the best costume…

CHICK. And the dance contest!

CLARISSA & DARLENE. Dance contest?

DARLENE. That's a new one.

CHICK. You know… for the boogiemen.

> (**CHICK** *does a few dance moves and then another "HA-CHA" after her joke.*)

DARLENE. So we've spotted our problem.

CLARISSA. Farmer Brown doesn't like Halloween and he's asleep in bed.

DARLENE. What are some possible solutions?

CHICK. We could wake him up.

CLARISSA. We could get him to arrive at the party not knowing it's the party.

CHICK. We could make sure it's a night he'll never forget.

DARLENE. That's it!

CHICK & CLARISSA. What?

DARLENE. All of those.

CHICK & CLARISSA. All of those?

[MUSIC NO. 07 – THE QUACKLE]

DARLENE. And I think I know just the tricky treat to use!

CHICK & CLARISSA. You do?

DARLENE. The Quackle.

CHICK & CLARISSA. The Quackle?!??!

DARLENE. Oh yes.
YOU SEE,
LONG AGO IN ANCIENT TRANSYLVANIA

THERE LIVED A FEATHERED FREAK THAT SHOOK
   ROMANIA
IT COMES OUT OF ITS LAIR EV'RY HALLOWEEN EVE
TO MAKE THE SEASON'S NONBELIEVERS MOST SURELY
   BELIEVE
THE LEGEND SAYS THIS CREATURE WAS A GHASTLY SIGHT,
FANGS AND SHARPENED CLAWS SURELY GAVE A FRIGHT
IT SEARCHES THROUGH THE NIGHT IN A CLOAK OF BLACK
CALLING TO THE MOON WITH "QUACK! QUACK! QUACK!"

IT'S THE QUACKLE
ITS WINGS SPREAD FAR AND WIDE
THE QUACKLE
AND A GOOGLY SPOOKY EYE
THE QUACKLE
YES, THE QUACKLE
IT'S THE QUACK, QUACK, CACKLE OF THE BEAST
KNOWN AS THE QUACKLE

THE VICTIMS OF THIS MONSTER TELL A CHILLING TALE
ALTHOUGH THEY TRIED TO FIGHT IT ALL ATTEMPTS
   WOULD FAIL
THE FLYING FIEND WOULD SHOW THEM HOW TO HAVE
   SOME FUN,
AND ON THIS SPECIAL NIGHT THE TRADITIONS BEGUN
SO SUDDENLY OCTOBER'S END WAS NEVER A MISS
HALLOWEEN BECAME THE PEOPLE'S HOLIDAY BLISS
THEY TRICKED AND TREATED, DANCED, AND BOBBED FOR
   APPLES ALL NIGHT
THEN THEY THANKED THE QUACKLE FOR MAKING IT
   RIGHT!

DARLENE.	CHICK & CLARISSA.
IT'S THE QUACKLE	
	OOH
ITS WINGS SPREAD FAR AND WIDE	

THE QUACKLE	OH
	AH
AND A GOOGLY	
SPOOKY EYE	
THE QUACKLE	
YES, THE QUACKLE	

DARLENE.

IT'S THE QUACK, QUACK, CACKLE OF THE BEAST
KNOWN AS THE QUACKLE

CHICK & CLARISSA.

THIS MONSTER ISN'T REALLY MEAN
IN FACT IT HATES TO HEAR US SCREAM
IT ONLY WANTS TO SPREAD AUTUMNAL CHEER

DARLENE.	**CHICK & CLARISSA.**
'CAUSE THE MOMENT	OOH
THAT WE LET	
OUR MONSTER ON	
THE LOOSE,	
FARMER BROWN WILL	AH
CHANGE HIS TUNE	
AND THEN HAVE NO	
EXCUSE	
OUR BOOGIE-BIRD IS	OH
SURE	
TO MAKE A CHANGE	
BEFORE THE FOULEST	OH
FOWL FLIES	
TO THE ROMANIAN	
RANGE	

CLARISSA, CHICK & DARLENE.

IT'S THE QUACKLE
ITS WINGS SPREAD FAR AND WIDE
THE QUACKLE
AND A GOOGLY SPOOKY EYE

    THE QUACKLE

    YES, THE QUACKLE

    IT'S THE QUACK, QUACK,

    CACKLE WHEN YOU HEAR IT CACKLE

    IT'S THE QUIRKY, KOOKY BEAST KNOWN AS THE QUACKLE

    THE QUACKLE

    IT'S THE QUACK, QUACK CACKLE OF THE BEAST KNOWN
        AS THE …

    WHAT???

    THE QUACKLE

CHICK. Where can we find this poultrygeist?

DARLENE. Leave its arrival to me.

       (**DARLENE** *starts to exit, then turns around.*)

But we'll need help summoning them.

CLARISSA. How do we do that?

DARLENE. You know how to tell them you're their friend.

       (**DARLENE** *exits.*)

CHICK. You don't think Darlene is being a Prankenstein,
do you?

CLARISSA. Not at all. She knows exactly what she's doing.
And we have everything we need to let The Quackle
know we're their friend.

CHICK. (*Realizing what to do.*) Ohhhhhhh. Then let's hit it!

      **[MUSIC NO. 07A – CALLING THE QUACKLE –
      PART 1]**

CHICK & CLARISSA.

    QUACKLE CAN YOU HEAR US? WE'RE A CALLIN'

    WE NEED YOU TO REPORT AND TO TAKE ON OUR CASE

    YOUR PRESENCE IS REQUESTED, WE HOPE YOU'RE
        FEELING RESTED

'CAUSE WHEN IT COMES TO CHANGIN' FOLKS, WE HEAR
    YOU'RE AN ACE
WE'RE HOPIN' THAT YOU'LL CLEVERLY
CHANGE OUR FARMER'S ENERGY
THE WELCOME MAT IS ROLLED OUT AND WAITING FOR YOU.

[MUSIC NO. 07B – CALLING THE QUACKLE – PART 2]

CHICK. Mice, we need your help again. The Quackle needs to hear that *you* are his friends. When I give the cue, I want you to go… *(Whatever fun rhythm works.)*
CREAK, CREAK, CREAK
CREAKIN' AT YOUR FEET
CREAK, CREAK, CREAK
CREAKIN' AT YOUR FEET

AUDIENCE MICE.
CREAK, CREAK, CREAK
CREAKIN' AT YOUR FEET
CREAK, CREAK, CREAK
CREAKIN' AT YOUR FEET

CLARISSA. Sheep, we're going to need your help as well. When I point you go…

(spoken in rhythm) "Crunch, crunch, crunchity crunch. Crunchin' as they eat."

AUDIENCE SHEEP.
CRUNCH, CRUNCH, CRUNCHITY CRUNCH
CRUNCHIN' AS THEY EAT
CRUNCH, CRUNCH, CRUNCHITY CRUNCH
CRUNCHIN' AS THEY EAT

CHICK. Your turn cats. When I point to you go…
TAPPY, TAPPY, TAPPY,
WITHOUT END. TIP TAP
TAPPY, TAPPY, TAPPY,
WITHOUT END. TIP TAP

AUDIENCE CATS.
> TAPPY, TAPPY, TAPPY,
> WITHOUT END. TIP TAP
> TAPPY, TAPPY, TAPPY,
> WITHOUT END. TIP TAP

DARLENE. Let's put them all together. 5...6...7...8...

> *(The **AUDIENCE MICE**, **AUDIENCE SHEEP** and **AUDIENCE CATS** shows The Quackle how friendly they are through their participation. The animal sound breakdown reaches a rhythmic, barnyard climax. **CLARISSA**, and **CHICK** continue singing.)*

CHICK & CLARISSA.
> THE MICE ARE CREAK, CREAK, CREAKIN' AT YOUR FEET
> THE SHEEP ARE CRUNCH, CRUNCH, CRUNCHIN' AS THEY EAT
> THE CATS ARE TAP, TAP, TAPPIN' WITHOUT END
> TELLIN' YOU THAT THEY'RE YOUR

> **(DARLENE** *[dressed as The Quackle, looking part vampire duck also part Phantom of the Opera] **flies in. The music quickly changes to Toccata in D, or another piece of spooky classical Halloween music.*)***

The Quackle!!!

DARLENE. *(As The Quackle. In a Bela Lugosi accent.)* I vant to have a Happy Halloveen!!!!

[MUSIC NO. 08 – CLICK, CLACK, BOO]

(A musical tag. The sound of thunder and lightning.)

---

* Performance Materials for *Click, Clack, Boo!* do not include music for this moment. A license to produce *Click, Clack, Boo!* does not include a performance license for any third-party or copyrighted recordings. Licensees should create their own.

(Another melody/rhythm starts slowly and begins to build faster and faster as it repeats. With each sound **CLARISSA** and **CHICK** make, **DARLENE** steps closer and closer to Farmer Brown's house.)*

CLARISSA. *(As **DARLENE** takes a step.)*
CLICK

CHICK. *(As **DARLENE** takes another step.)*
CLACK

DARLENE. *(Stopping in her tracks and striking a pose.)*
BOO!

CLARISSA. *(As **DARLENE** takes another step.)*
CLICK

CHICK. *(As **DARLENE** takes another step.)*
CLACK

DARLENE. *(Stopping in her tracks and striking a pose.)*
BOO!

CLARISSA. *(As **DARLENE** takes a step.)*
CLICK

CHICK. *(As **DARLENE** takes another step.)*
CLACK

DARLENE. *(Stopping in her tracks and striking a pose.)*
BOO!

FARMER BROWN. *(Stirring in his bed.)* Is that the rooster? Morning already?

CLARISSA. *(As **DARLENE** takes a step.)*
CLICK

---

* Performance Materials for *Click, Clack, Boo!* do not include music for this moment. A license to produce *Click, Clack, Boo!* does not include a performance license for any third-party or copyrighted recordings. Licensees should create their own.

CHICK. *(As **DARLENE** takes another step.)*
CLACK

DARLENE. *(Stopping in her tracks and striking a pose.)*
BOO!

CLARISSA. *(As **DARLENE** takes another step.)*
CLICK

CHICK. *(As **DARLENE** takes another step.)*
CLACK

DARLENE. *(Stopping in her tracks and striking a pose.)*
BOO!

CLARISSA. *(As **DARLENE** takes a step.)*
CLICK

CHICK. *(As **DARLENE** takes another step.)*
CLACK

DARLENE. *(Stopping in her tracks and striking a pose.)*
BOO!

FARMER BROWN. *(Pulling the sheet up and shaking.)* No. That's a different sound in the crisp night air.

CLARISSA. *(As **DARLENE** takes another step.)*
CLICK

CHICK. *(As **DARLENE** takes another step.)*
CLACK

DARLENE. *(Stopping in her tracks and striking a pose.)*
BOO!

FARMER BROWN. It's coming closer…

CLARISSA. *(As **DARLENE** takes a step.)*
CLICK

CHICK. *(As **DARLENE** takes another step.)*
CLACK

DARLENE. *(Stopping in her tracks and striking a pose.)*
BOO!

FARMER BROWN. And closer!

CLARISSA. *(As **DARLENE** takes another step.)*
CLICK

CHICK. *(As **DARLENE** takes another step.)*
CLACK

DARLENE. *(Stopping in her tracks and striking a pose.)*
BOO!

CLARISSA. *(As **DARLENE** takes a step.)*
CLICK

CHICK. *(As **DARLENE** takes another step.)*
CLACK

DARLENE. *(Stopping in her tracks and striking a pose.)*
BOO!

CLARISSA. *(As **DARLENE** takes another step.)*
CLICK

CHICK. *(As **DARLENE** takes another step.)*
CLACK

DARLENE. *(Stopping in her tracks and striking a pose.)*
BOO!

FARMER BROWN. It's on the front porch!

CLARISSA, CHICK & DARLENE.
CLICK

FARMER BROWN.
CLACK?

CLARISSA, CHICK & DARLENE.
CLICK, CLICK

FARMER BROWN.
CLACK, CLACK?

CHICK.
BOO!

CLARISSA, CHICK & DARLENE.
> CLICK, CLICK

FARMER BROWN.
> CLACK, CLACK

CLARISSA, CHICK & DARLENE.
> CLICK, CLACK, BOOOOOOOOOOOOOOOOOOOO!

> *(End of intro. A change of tempo with the verse.)*

CLARISSA & CHICK.
> YOU'VE BEEN ASLEEP
> COUTNING YOUR SHEEP
> FORGETTING ABOUT OUR BASH

DARLENE. *(As The Quackle.)*
> BUT I'VE COME TO REMIND YOU
> THAT YOU'VE BEEN SO BLIND
> TO TAKE PART IN OUR MONSTER MASH!

CLARISSA, CHICK & DARLENE.
> CLICK, CLACK, CLICK, CLACK, BOO
> CLICK, CLACK, CLICK, CLACK, BOO!
> CLICK, CLACK, CLICK CLACK CLICK CLACK BOO
> CLICK CLACK CLICK CLACK …

FARMER BROWN.
> SHOO! SHOO!
> CLICK CLACK CLICK CLACK CLICK CLACK BOO

CLARISSA & CHICK.
> WE ARE YOUR GALS
> YOUR HALLOWEEN PALS
> AND YOU ARE THE V.I.P.

DARLENE. *(As The Quackle.)*
> COME ON GET UP
> LET'S GO GET OUT
> LET'S GET HALLOWEENY

CLARISSA, CHICK & DARLENE.
    CLICK, CLACK, CLICK, CLACK BOO
    CLICK, CLACK, CLICK, CLACK

FARMER BROWN.
    SHOO! SHOO!

CLARISSA, CHICK & DARLENE.
    CLICK, CLACK, CLICK CLACK CLICK CLACK BOO
    CLICK CLACK CLICK CLACK …

FARMER BROWN.
    SHOO! SHOO!
    WHAT IS THIS,
    WHO ARE YOU?
    I DON'T MUCH LIKE THIS SHOCK
    OR MUCH OF ANYTHING THAT'S NEW
    I'M FRIGHTENED TO THE BONE,
    PLEASE LEAVE ME ALONE!

(Dance break. **DARLENE** *[dressed as The Quackle], lurches forward.* **FARMER BROWN** *leaps out of bed. The Quackle pursues* **FARMER BROWN** *until he has left his house and traveled out into the barnyard.)*

CLARISSA & CHICK.	**FARMER BROWN.**
CLICK CLACK	
CLICK CLACK BOO	I DON'T
CLICK CLACK CLICK CLACK BOO	WANT YOUR ATTENTION
CLICK CLACK CLICK CLACK	I DON'T
CLICK CLACK BOO	WANT IT AT
CLICK CLACK CLICK CLACK BOO	ALL!
	WHAT IS THAT
CLICK CLACK CLICK CLACK	THING???
BOO	WHY

CLICK CLACK CLICK
   CLACK
CLICK CLACK CLICK
   CLACK BOO!

IS IT
HERE!

> *(At the end of the number,* **CLARISSA**, **CHICK**
> *and* **DARLENE** *have put up a huge invitation/*
> *sign that says "Halloween party at the barn!"*
> *and disappeared, behind it?* **FARMER BROWN**
> *addresses the barnyard [Audience].)*

FARMER BROWN. I've never seen anything like that creature in my entire life. Why, it's so ugly, if it threw a boomerang it wouldn't come back.

> *(Takes a moment to think and then.)*

It's so ugly, it would make onions cry.

> *(Takes another moment.)*

It's so ugly it would have to trick-or-treat over the phone.

DARLENE. *(Appearing quickly from behind the invite.)* You're no Prince Charming yourself, Farmer…

> *(A hand/wing quickly appears and yanks* **DARLENE** *back behind the invitation.* **FARMER BROWN** *notices the huge invite.)*

FARMER BROWN. I feel like I've been done bit, chewed up, and spit out.

> *(The sound of crickets and perhaps other sounds of the night.)*

What am I doing out here on Halloween night? I should be back home hittin' the hay!

> *(The croak of a bullfrog.)*

I'm glad you agree Mr. Bullfrog.

(*The sound of a hound dog.*)

You too, Mr. Hound Dog.

(*The mysterious growl of an unidentified creature is heard, like a duck?* **FARMER BROWN** *turns pale.*)

I'm sorry. I didn't quite catch that, Mr. …

(**FARMER BROWN** *turns even paler as the mysterious growl of an unidentified creature is heard again, like a duck?*)

Mr. …

(**FARMER BROWN** *is terrified as the mysterious growl of an unidentified creature is heard again.*)

Like my mama always said, "The only thing we have to fear is fear *and* monsters!" I gotta get out of here…

(*Turning around, looking for a place to go, he sees the invite.*)

In all my born days!

(*Reading.*)

Halloween party at the barn!

[MUSIC NO. 8A – NONSENSE (REPRISE)]

(*Out to the audience.*)

Don't they know, there ain't no education in the second kick of the mule. This just sticks in my craw. I've told you…

I DON'T LIKE HALLOWEEN PARTIES
YOU CAN'T CHANGE MY MIND
WHEN INVITES SHOW, I HIT THE ROAD
AND LEAVE ALL THAT BEHIND

NO, I DON'T LIKE HALLOWEEN PARTIES

ALL THOSE SUG'RY TREATS … BLECH!

WON'T BLOW MY HORN FOR CANDY CORN

OR ANYTHING TOO SWEET!

SPECTERS GIVE ME GOOSEBUMPS

ZOMBIES GO ON AND MOAN

SOULLESS SOULS, MUMMIES, AND TROLLS I LIKE IT ON
   MY OWN!

NO! I DON'T LIKE HALLOWEEN PARTIES

I DON'T LIKE THEM AT ALL

ALL THE FLAPDOODLE BOSH SLITHY GALOSH

IT'S ALL NONSENSE TO …

> *(Another mysterious growl of an unidentified creature is heard again.)*

Swat at my hind with a melon rind! I gotta get out of here!

> *(He screams.)*

AHHHHHHHHH!!!!

> *(**FARMER BROWN** excitedly runs right into the huge invite, topples, and pulls it down revealing **CLARISSA**, **DARLENE**, and **CHICK**.)*

CLARISSA, CHICK & DARLENE. Welcome!

CLARISSA. So glad you could make it to the Halloween Hop.

CHICK. In fact, you're just in time for the contest results!

FARMER BROWN. Contests?!?!? Oh never mind those. I never win.

DARLENE. And the winner of the loudest scream contest is…

FARMER BROWN. Not me.

DARLENE. *(Holding out a big ribbon.)* Farmer Brown!

FARMER BROWN. *(Looking out from under the big sign/ invite.)* What?

CLARISSA. And the winner of the most spirited guest is…

FARMER BROWN. Can't be me.

CLARISSA. *(Holding out a big ribbon.)* Farmer Brown!

FARMER BROWN. *(Overwhelmed.)* My stars and garters! Are you sure?

CHICK. And the winner of the best costume contest is…

> *(Holding out a big ribbon.)*

Is…

> *(Continues to hold out the big ribbon.)*

DARLENE. Chick, what's wrong?

CHICK. I don't have an envelope to announce the winner.

CLARISSA. *(Pulling one out, getting something together.)* Here.

CHICK. The winner is…

> *(Drumroll. **CHICK** opens the envelope and announces.)*

Farmer Brown!

FARMER BROWN. Me? I won? First place?

CHICK. You sure did. I won first place in the costume contest for years.

FARMER BROWN. As what?

CHICK. A hotdog. I was really on a roll.

FARMER BROWN. But I'm not wearing a costume.

CHICK. Nonsense. I'm definitely picking up some high fashion vibes here. Don't you think so Clarissa?

CLARISSA. I sure do, Chick. What do you think, Darlene?

DARLENE. I definitely think Farmer Brown is an original in that ensemble, worthy of first prize.

CHICK. *(To* **FARMER BROWN**.*)* Knock, knock…

DARLENE. *(Touching* **FARMER BROWN***'s shoulder.)* Brace yourself.

FARMER BROWN. Who's there?

CHICK. Wooden.

FARMER BROWN. Wooden who?

CHICK. Wouldn't you like to hear another knock, knock joke?

FARMER BROWN. Sure.

CHICK. Knock, knock.

FARMER BROWN. Who's there?

CHICK. Waiter.

FARMER BROWN. Waiter, who?

CHICK. Waiter minute I got another knock, knock joke for you.

DARLENE. I warned you.

CHICK. Knock, knock.

FARMER BROWN. Who's there?

CHICK. Winner.

FARMER BROWN. Winner, who?

CHICK. Winner, you!

FARMER BROWN. Me? I might have screamed the loudest and I might been the most spirited, but to win a costume contest? I'm not wearing anything special?

DARLENE. Anything special?!?!?

CLARISSA. You're *you* aren't you?

FARMER BROWN. Yes.

[MUSIC NO. 09 – BE FREE]

CLARISSA. That alone is worth many, many awards…

NO MATTER WHAT YOU WEAR

OR HOW YOU DRESS

CLARISSA & DARLENE.

HOW YOU DRESS

CLARISSA.

YOU ARE SURE TO STAND OUT

SHOW YOUR FLAIR

AND BE A SUCCESS

CLARISSA & DARLENE.

BE A SUCCESS

DARLENE.

YOU GOT THAT SPECIAL THING THAT LIVES INSIDE

NO NEED TO BE AFRAID, GO ON AND SHOW YOUR PRIDE

CHICK.

NOBODY CAN TELL YOU WHAT TO DO

EMBRACE IT! LOVE IT! JUST BE YOU!

CLARISSA, CHICK & DARLENE.

YOUR STAR IS BRIGHT AND IT LOOKS SO FINE

DON'T PUT IT OUT. LET IT SHINE, SHINE, SHINE …

BE YOU

BE FREE

ALWAYS BE YOURSELF, ANSWER CANDIDLY

BE YOU

BE FREE

EMBRACE YOUR VERY OWN INDIVIDUALITY

BE YOU

STAY TRUE

BE FREE
BE FREE
BE FREE
BE FREE
BE FREE

FARMER BROWN.

I NEVER THOUGHT I WAS MUCH OF A WINNER
I KEPT MY HEAD DOWN AND FOUND A PLACE TO HIDE
THINGS HAVE TURNED AROUND AND I SEE HOPE START
TO GLIMMER
I FEEL SO HAPPY HAVING FRIENDS BY MY SIDE
AND NOW YOU'RE TELLING ME THAT I'M THE TOP OF THE
PACK
AND MY SILLY SOLITARY LIFE WELL, I'LL NEVER LOOK
BACK!

CLARISSA, CHICK & DARLENE.

WE'RE GLAD YOU SEE YOU ARE NOT A CHORE
YOUR PRICE IS HIGH, YOU'RE WORTH MORE, MORE,
MORE!
BE YOU
BE FREE
ALWAYS BE YOURSELF, ANSWER CANDIDLY
BE YOU
BE FREE
EMBRACE YOUR VERY OWN INDIVIDUALITY
BE YOU
STAY TRUE
BE FREE
BE FREE
BE FREE
BE FREE
BE FREE

DARLENE. OK barnyard friends, we're about to celebrate
the night away, but before we leave you.

We have three simple things that we want you to remember and they go like this…

CLARISSA, CHICK & DARLENE.

ONE!

CHICK.

YOU HAVE A VOICE
NEVER LET IT FADE AWAY

CLARISSA, CHICK & DARLENE.

TWO!

CLARISSA.

YOU HAVE A CHOICE
EVEN WHEN YOU ARE AFRAID

CLARISSA, CHICK & DARLENE.

THREE!

DARLENE.

YOU'RE ENOUGH. LET NOBODY GET YOU DOWN.
YOU'RE THE PRIZE AND HERE'S YOUR CROWN…

CLARISSA.

HERE'S YOUR CROWN …

CLARISSA & DARLENE

CROWN…

CHICK.

HERE'S YOUR CROWN …

CLARISSA, CHICK & DARLENE.

CROWN!
BE YOU
BE FREE
ALWAYS BE YOURSELF, ANSWER CANDIDLY
BE YOU
BE FREE
EMBRACE YOUR VERY OWN INDIVIDUALITY
BE YOU

STAY TRUE
BE FREE
BE FREE
BE FREE
BE FREE
BE FREE
FREE!

BE YOU
BE FREE
ALWAYS BE YOURSELF, ANSWER CANDIDLY
BE YOU
BE FREE
EMBRACE YOUR VERY OWN INDIVIDUALITY
BE YOU
STAY TRUE
BE FREE
BE FREE
BE FREE
BE FREE
BE FREE
BE FREE (BE YOU)
BE YOU (BE FREE)
BE FREE (BE YOU)
BE YOU
FREE!

FARMER BROWN. *(Celebrating.)* I'm a winner! I'm a winner!

DARLENE. You are indeed. And as winner of three contests, you're also the winner of a special prize.

FARMER BROWN. *(Shocked.)* I am?

DARLENE. Drum roll please…

> (**DARLENE** *presents another envelope or box to* **FARMER BROWN** *who opens the envelope or box and reads.)*

FARMER BROWN. A herd of alpacas!

CHICK. Now that's my kind of prize.

CLARISSA. Look at that. Farmer Brown wins a prize and your wish came true, Chick.

CHICK. I'll be so fleeced to meet them.

FARMER BROWN. Thank you, ladies. This has been very special. I've never won anything my entire life.

DARLENE. That's not true, Farmer Brown. You won our friendship long ago.

FARMER BROWN. *(Touched.)* Well now, that's the best prize I could have ever received.

DARLENE. Friends and togetherness is the true spirit of any holiday, including Halloween.

FARMER BROWN. You're so right. I have you. Who needs ribbons when I have that?

CHICK. If you don't want the ribbons…

FARMER BROWN. Step back, chicken!

> (**CHICK** *jumps back.*)

I'm gonna be loud…

And proud…

And at a Halloween Party!

[MUSIC NO. 10 – HALLOWEEN HOP (REPRISE)]

CLARISSA.
I'LL START THE DANCIN'

DARLENE.
I'LL GREET THE GUESTS

CHICK.
TONIGHT I'M TELLING YOU IS GONNA BE THE BEST!

DARLENE.

I FOUND THE MONSTERS

CHICK.

I FOUND THE GHOSTS

CLARISSA.

I THINK THE FOUR OF US MAKE PERFECT HOSTS

CLARISSA, CHICK & DARLENE.

IT'S OUR FAVORITE TIME OF YEAR
WHEN THE AIR IS CRISP AND OUR FRIENDS ARE HERE,
WE'RE GONNA MAKE THE BARNYARD BOP
TONIGHT AT OUR HALLOWEEN HOP!
HOP HOP HOP HOP
HALLA HALLA HALLA HALLA HALLOWEEN HOP
WE'RE GONNA MAKE THE BARNYARD BOP

WE'LL BE DANCIN' TILL WE CANNOT STOP
THIS JOLLY JOYFUL WACKY HOOPLA'S GONNA POP!

CHICK.

CANDY AT HALLOWEEN

DARLENE.

COSTUMES AT HALLOWEEN

CLARISSA.

PARTYING AT HALLOWEEN

FARMER BROWN.

FRIENDSHIP AT HALLOWEEN

CLARISSA, CHICK, DARLENE AND FARMER BROWN.

WE LOVE HALLOWEEN! TONIGHT AT OUR HALLOWEEN
    HOP!!!!
BOO! HOP!

[MUSIC NO. 11 – BOWS]

End of Play

9 780573 711121